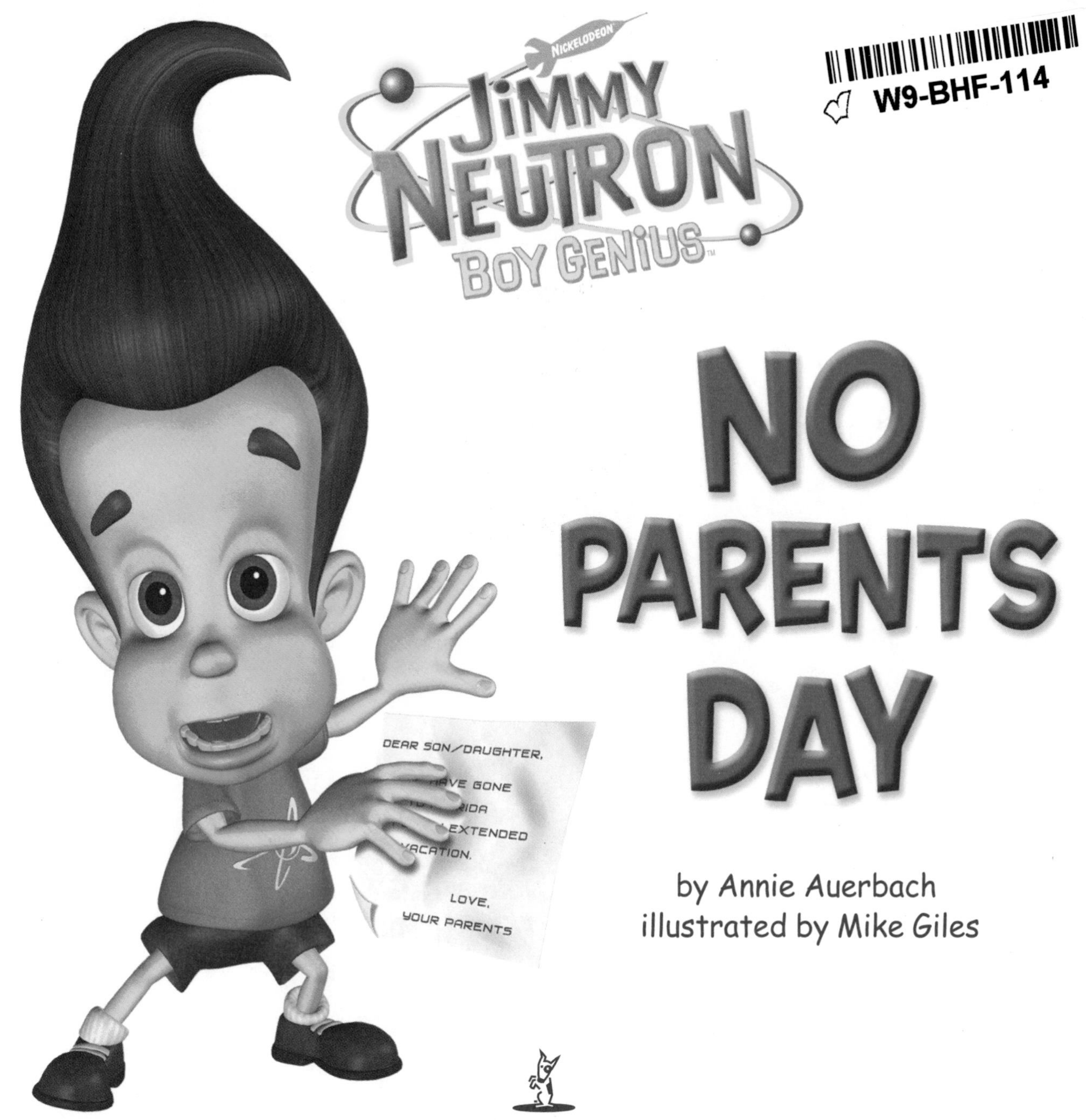

NO PARENTS DAY

by Annie Auerbach
illustrated by Mike Giles

Simon Spotlight/Nickelodeon
New York London Toronto Sydney Singapore

Special thanks to Manny Galan
Pencils by Kelsey Shannon

SIMON SPOTLIGHT
An imprint of Simon & Schuster Children's Publishing Division
1230 Avenue of the Americas, New York, New York 10020

Manufactured in the United States of America
First Edition
2 4 6 8 10 9 7 5 3 1
ISBN 0-689-84541-3

A very strange thing happened one night in Retroville. . . .

The next morning Jimmy Neutron discovered that his parents were gone. They had left a note on the refrigerator.

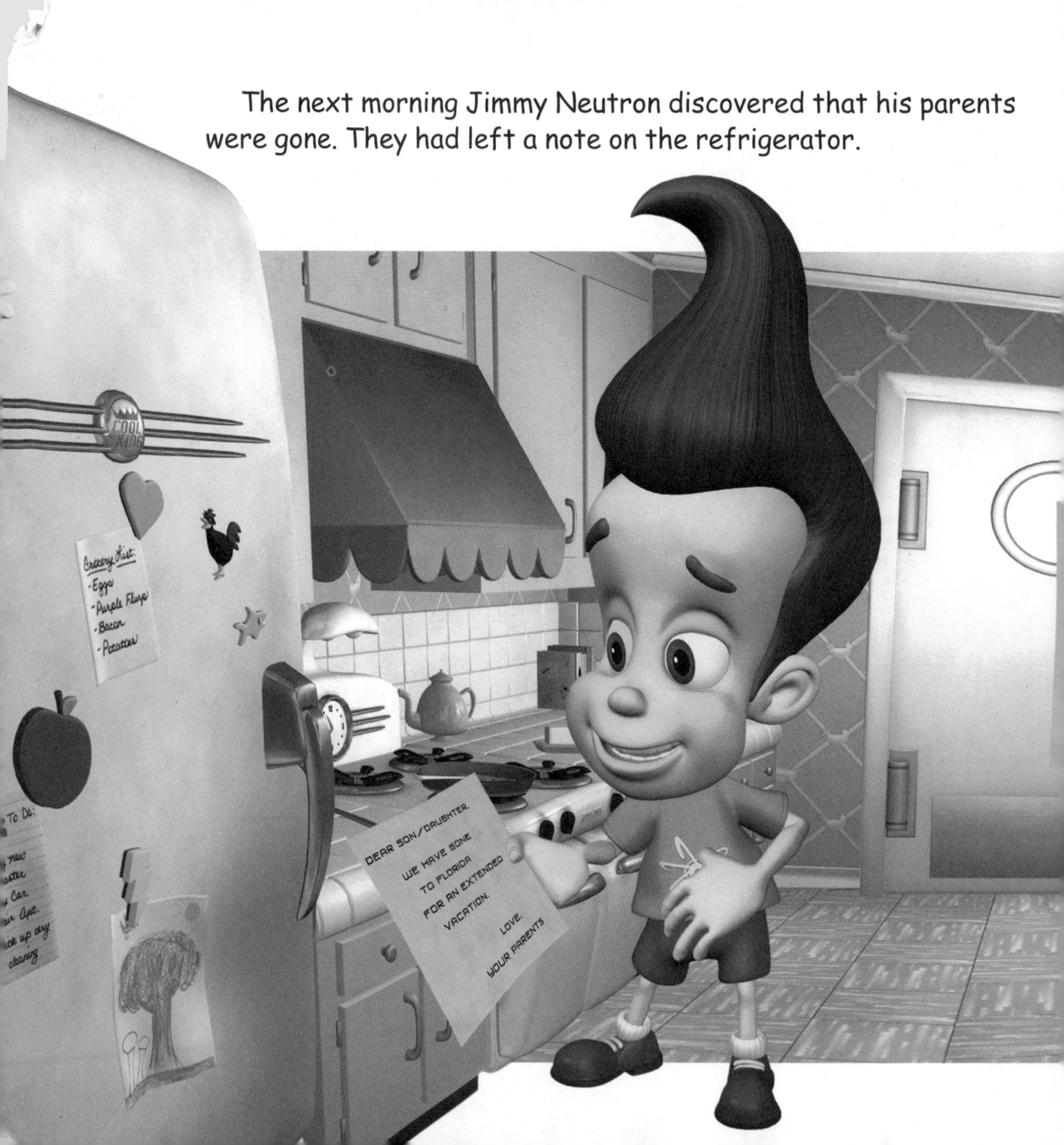

Jimmy's best friends, Carl and Sheen, had found the same notes from their parents.

"NO PARENTS?!" Jimmy cheered. "Jumpin' Jupiter! This is going to be the best day ever!"

TOYS
Ages 4 & Up
ASTRO RANGER
SUGAR QUACKS
SUGAR QUACKS
QUACKER
FREE TOY

Jimmy and his friends headed to their favorite ice-cream shop. Sheen lobbed a scoop of strawberry ice cream high into the air just as Cindy Vortex and her friend Libby walked in the door.

Sheen ducked down in his seat. "Ooops!"

"Now, that's what I call playing with your food!" Jimmy said.

"Hey, Cindy! Where can I get a hairdo like that?" Jimmy asked.

"You already have one!" Cindy scoffed, wiping her hair. "What's the matter, Neutron, can't have any fun without your parents around?"

"Far from it! Now that our parents are away, the boys and I are about to have some serious fun! We're going to Retroland," replied Jimmy.

"Oh, yeah?" Cindy said. "Race ya!"

"Let the games begin!" Sheen shouted in his best Ultra Lord superhero voice.

"I bet we can ride the Bat Outta Heck ride more times than you, Ultra Dorks," Cindy challenged.

"You're on!" the boys cried.

BAT OUTT
HECK

"This is so cool!" Jimmy said after their seventeenth ride in a row. "No buying tickets. No waiting in line. We don't even have to get out of the car!"

Carl reached into his pocket for his inhaler. He wheezed and sputtered as he said, "Num . . . ber . . . se . . . ven . . . teen . . ."

Several cotton candies later Carl was feeling better. Sticky pink fluff coated his mouth. And his fingers. And his hair.

Jimmy watched as Cindy tried to keep up with Carl. "I guess the Lose Your Lunch ride is out of the question, huh, Cindy?"

"Please don't mention lunch," Cindy groaned.

After taking one too many turns on the Pain in the Neck ride, ripping his shirt on a turnstile, and eating a funny-tasting hot dog, Jimmy walked home alone. "Pukin' Pluto!" he moaned. "This is the worst day ever!"

And then it struck him. Why would all of the parents go away at the same time? Jimmy headed straight to his secret lab.

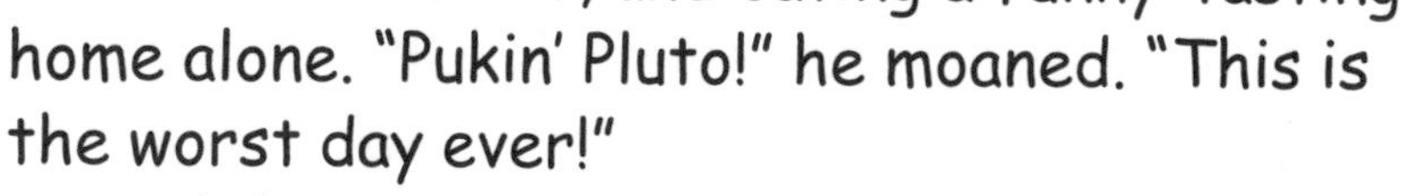

On a hunch Jimmy fed the note his parents had left through his handwriting-analysis machine. "Holy Moon Pie!" he cried. "This note's a fake!"

Just then he noticed a blinking light on his long-range Space Scanner.

"Alien alert? Now, why would aliens be—" Jimmy gasped. "That's it! Aliens have stolen our parents!"

Later that night Jimmy and his friends gathered in his backyard.

"So there you have it," he concluded. "Our parents are at the mercy of evil aliens. And one thing's for sure, we need our parents—and now they need us!"

"But how are we going to save them, Jimmy?" asked Carl, sounding worried.

"With this!" said Jimmy, pointing to his most important invention. "I've reworked a Retroland rocket ride for the mission. Goddard, initiate launch sequence!"

"It's up!" cheered Carl. SPLAT! "It's down."

"Nice try, Neutron," Cindy snickered.

Jimmy tried to figure out what had gone wrong. "Think, think," he muttered. "I need more power, so I've got to find plutonium, but—"

"Why didn't you just say so?" asked Cindy. "There's plenty of plutonium over at the power plant."

Jimmy's eyes lit up. "Eureka!"

"Now, if you'll just hand over the plutonium," Jimmy said when the girls returned, "the boys and I will be on our way to save our parents."

"Not so fast, big hair!" cried Cindy. "If the plutonium goes, we go."

"Girls on a space mission?" Jimmy wrinkled his nose. "Oh, all right. But only for our parents' sake."

The spaceships took shape under Jimmy's direction.

Soon the kids turned the Retroland Amusement Park rides into the spectacular Retroville space fleet.

Jimmy inspected the lineup.

"We're ready."

Goddard's digital voice counted down, "Five . . . four . . . three . . . two . . . one . . . we have liftoff!"

Suddenly the night sky was bright with fiery rockets. Jimmy raised his fist in the air. "Let's go get our parents!"

Before long everything was back to normal in Retroville. At least for now . . .